First Edition

Design by *ACT! Graphixs*

Library of Congress Catalog-In-Publication Data:

Donovan, Rosalind.
    Come To My Island/Rosalind Donovan:paintings by Bruce Smith.
            p.   cm.
    Summary: Illustrations and rhyming text invite the reader to experience life on a Caribbean Island.
    ISBN 1-881316-30-0.   ISBN 1-881316-47-5
    [1. Caribbean Area Fiction.   2. Stories in rhyme.] I. Smith, Bruce. ill. II. Title.
    PZ8.3.D7237C0 1996   96-3495
    [E] --dc20   CIP
                                                                                            AC

                    10 9 8 7 6 5 4 3 2

printed and bound in the United States.

Published by
A&B Publishers Group
1000 Atlantic Avenue
Brooklyn, New York 11238

COME TO MY ISLAND

A&B PUBLISHERS GROUP
Brooklyn, New York
11238

Come to my island. Come with me

So many wonderful things to see

We'll sail on the blue Caribbean Sea

We'll run on the beach from dusk to dawn

And watch the sun rise in the early morn

Come to my island. Come with me

We'll eat fruits from the mango tree

FISH
Water
today

We'll feast on saltfish and fungi

We'll take a ride on a little donkey

And visit the shops in Redcliffe Quay

We'll see grown-ups chat over tea.

We'll watch a shipwright chopping a "knee."

We'll see school children dressed uniformly

And Listen to stories about sly Anansi

Come to my island. Come with me

We'll tickle auntie's new brown baby

We'll see baskets balanced perfectly

We'll dance the limbo at a wedding party

And "jump-up" at carnival and shout with glee

Come to my island. Come with me

We'll hear the steel drums playing loudly

We'll sing calypsoes so merrily

Calypsonian Competition

We'll watch the sun set so beautifully

Oh how happy we will be.

ABOUT THE AUTHOR

Rosalind Donovan has had a joyful and rewarding career in elementary education within the New York City public school system. She has been a teacher in the Harlem community for over twenty-five years, during which time she taught grades 2 through 5. In 1980 Ms. Donovan took a sabbatical leave and earned a second master's degree in special education. She continued her career as a teacher of learning disabled youngsters. She also taught English as a second language. During the last three years of her career she worked as a staff developer. This enabled her to become a mentor to a new generation of teachers and allowed her the opportunity to past on her enthusiasm for teaching to this new generation. Ms. Donovan retired in 1991 and still currently lives in New York City. However, she tries to spend as much time as possible in the island of Antigua, West Indies.

Come To My Island represents a lifelong desire to introduce young readers to the beauty of the Caribbean through the wonderful world of books.

ABOUT THE ARTIST

Bruce Smith is a self-taught artist whose colorful paintings reflect the charm of the Caribbean. He lives with his family on a small sailing boat that he built himself. He frequently sails to most of the Caribbean Islands. However, his favorites islands are those small remote ones, where boats are still hand-built and people's lifestyles remain simple.

Exhibitions:

1994 Sunny Caribbee Art Gallery, Tortola; Greenwith Gallery, Phillipsburg, St. Maarten; Spencer-Cameron Gallery, St. Kitts.

1993 Nevis Gallery of Art, Nevis; Mango Tango Gallery, St. Thomas; U.S. Virgin Islands. La Gallerie, St. Barts;. Harmony Hall, Antigua. The Four Seasons Resort, Nevis; Harmony Hall, Jamaica.

1992 Gallery 20, St. Barts; Here Today Gallery, St. Barts; Greenwith Gallery, St. Maarten; La Gallerie, St. Bart; City Hall Gallery, Hamilton, Bermuda; Mosalcs Association Show, City Hall Gallery. Bermuda; One-man show, Harmony Hall, Antigua.

1991 St. Barts Regatta Art Show, St. Barts; Parrot Cage Gallery, Nevis; Prinderella's Restaurant, Nevis; Nevis Gallery of Art.

1974-1980 Mural painting on the Caribbean Islands of St. Maarten, Antigua, Tortola, St. Barts, Dominica, Grenada.

GLOSSARY

Anansi- This West African folklore figure was both a man and a spider. When things were going well he was a man but when in trouble he took the form of a spider. Anansi was clever and loved to play tricks on the animals. West Africans brought these delightful stories with them when they were brought to the Caribbean as slaves. Even today, in the Caribbean Islands, old women gather the children when the sun goes down and tell these wonderful stories.

Calypso- This is a type of folk music that originated in the Caribbean islands. African slaves who were brought to Trinidad to work on plantations were forbidden to speak to one another. Therefore, they used these songs to communicate feelings and information. Today the words of calypsoes may express political views, current events and gossip.

Caribbean sea- This is a body of water that is part of the Atlantic ocean, lying between the West Indies and Central and South America.

Carnival- This is a festival that features feasting and merrymaking. In ancient times, this festival was held before lent. Carnivals in the Caribbean feature elaborate costumes, troops of dancers, steel bands and hundreds of revelers parading the streets.

Fungi- (Pronounced Fungee) This is a food that is made with yellow cornmeal and water. Fungi is often eaten with okra and cod fish.

Jump-up- This is the term used to describe the dancing that goes on during carnival.

Knee- This is a curved piece of wood, usually white cedar, that is used to strengthen and support wooden vessels.

Limbo- This is a dance performed in the Caribbean. Dancers pass under a stick that is gradually lowered as the dancer passes under the stick with his body extended backwards. This dance, like so many other Caribbean culture, originated in Africa.

Mango- This is a yellowish, red tropical fruit with a firm skin and a hard central stone. It is juicy and delicious to eat.

Quay- This is a stretch of paved bank or a solid artificial landing place near water, providing a convenient place for ships to load and unload. It is pronounced like "key."

Salt fish- This is salted cod fish prepared in a tomato sauce and often eaten with fungi.

Shipwright- This is a carpenter who is skilled in constructing and repairing wooden ships.

CHILDREN'S TITLES

Fun With Series

Fun with Numbers	3.95
Fun with Letters	3,95
Fun with Colors	3.95
Fun with Shapes	3.95

Afrotots

Afrotots ABC	3.95
Afrotots 123	3.95

Other Titles

When I Look In The Miror	6.95
When I Look In THe Mirror Coloring & Activity	2.95
Come To My Island	7.95
Prayers & Meditations for our Little Angels	8.95
Melanin & Me	6.95

Little Zeng Series

Little Zeng's ABC	4.95
Little Zeng's Ancient Egypt	2.95
Little Zeng's Hannibal	2.95
Little Zeng in Zimbabwe	2.95
Little Zeng goes to Harlem	2.95

Our Books make excellent gifts
Send for a gift Certificate and our complete catalog

A&B Publishers Group
1000 Atlantic Avenue
Brooklyn, New York, 11238